Red-spotted
Newt

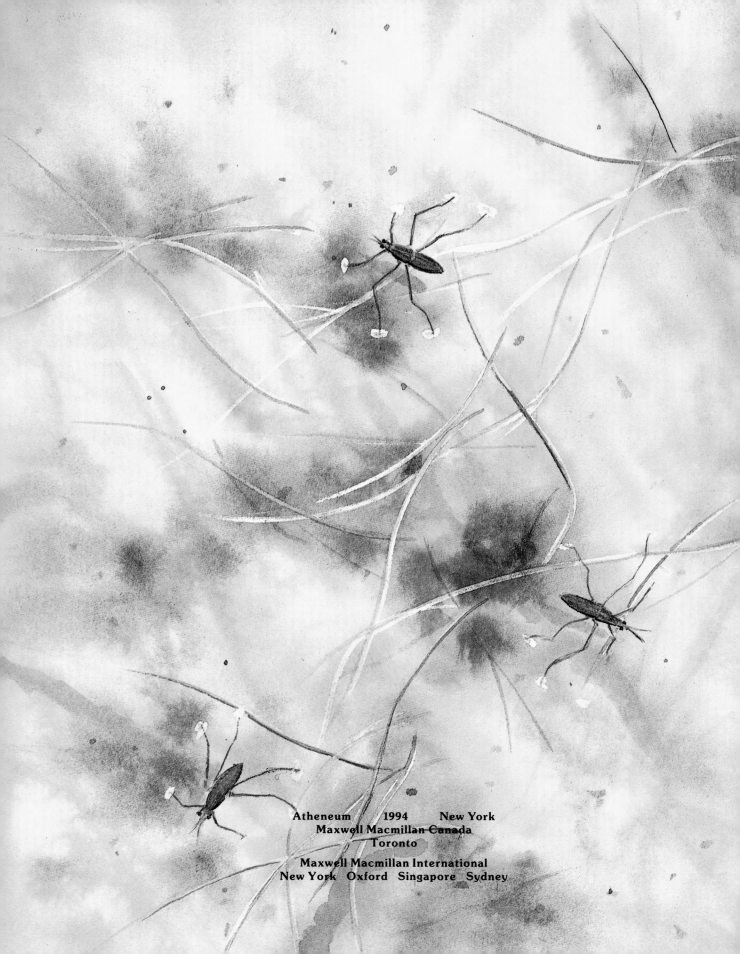

Atheneum   1994   New York
Maxwell Macmillan Canada
Toronto

Maxwell Macmillan International
New York Oxford Singapore Sydney

Red-spotted Newt

by **Doris Gove**

illustrated by **Beverly Duncan**

The author thanks Dr. Richard Bruce, Dr. Gordon Burghardt,
Gale Lawrence, and Dr. Paul Verrell for helpful comments.

For my children and the red efts that we have found on wet, woodsy walks
B.K.D.

Observations of newts were made at the Highlands Biological
Station of the University of North Carolina and at Norris, Tennessee.

Atheneum
Macmillan Publishing Company
866 Third Avenue
New York, NY 10022

Maxwell Macmillan Canada, Inc.
1200 Eglinton Avenue East
Suite 200
Don Mills, Ontario M3C 3N1

Macmillan Publishing Company is part of the Maxwell Communication Group of Companies.

First edition
Printed in Hong Kong
10 9 8 7 6 5 4 3 2 1

The text of this book is set in Souvenir.
The illustrations are rendered in watercolors.
Printed on recycled paper

Library of Congress Cataloging-in-Publication Data

Gove, Doris.
Red-spotted newt / by Doris Gove; illustrated by Beverly Duncan.
—1st ed.
p.   cm.
Summary: Describes the physical characteristics, life cycle, and
behavior of the red-spotted newt.
ISBN 0–689–31697–6
1. Notophthalmus viridescens—Life cycles—Juvenile literature.
[1. Newts.] I. Duncan, Beverly, 1947–   ill. II. Title.
QL668.C28G78   1994
597.6′5—dc20   91–34497

A newt rose to the surface of a small pond in the woods. She took a gulp of air and swam back to the muddy bottom with a few strong tail strokes. Her skin was greenish brown, and she had a row of bright red spots along each side. Her body was heavy with eggs.

She pushed at the mud with her nose, creeping forward, until she came to the stem of a water weed. She twisted her body up around it, grasped the stem with both hind feet, and laid a brown egg surrounded by clear jelly. She pushed the jelly against the stem until it stuck fast, and she pulled the end of a leaf down with her hind legs to make a tunnel around the egg. Then she swam to the bottom, nosing at the mud and a few rotting sticks. She found some tiny clams and ate them.

It was the end of April, and she had already laid several eggs, some on stems, some underneath sticks or rocks, and some in leaf curl nests. Her body still held more than one hundred eggs, and she would search out hiding places for them one at a time for the next three months. She folded her legs back against her body and swam away through the cloudy water. Spring sunlight warmed the pond and lit up the bright green new leaves on the tall trees around it.

Red-spotted newts are salamanders that live in the eastern United States and southeastern Canada. They lead a more complicated life than most salamanders or other amphibians like frogs and toads: When they grow out of the tadpole, or larva, stage, they wander through the forest for one to five years. Then they return to the marsh or pond where they hatched and take up life in the water again. During the wandering land stage of their lives, red-spotted newts are called efts, and they are most active in rainy or foggy weather. Like other amphibians, they need to stay in damp places so that their skins can absorb oxygen. Efts look so different from the adult newts that live in the water that biologists once thought they were two different kinds of salamanders.

Most amphibians lay their eggs in clumps or strings, and the tadpoles hatch together and live together. But newts lay their eggs one at a time, far apart, and over a period of two or three months. When newt larvae hatch, they seem to keep up the habit of being alone; if they meet other newts, they move away.

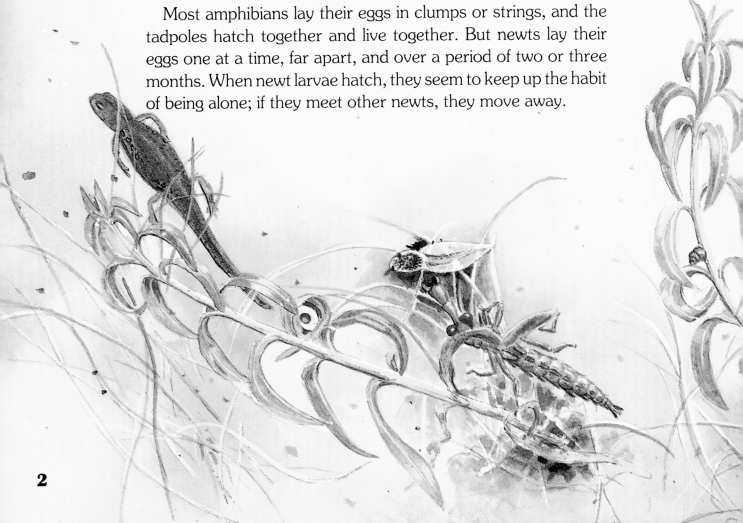

The little round newt egg inside its jelly stayed brown on top but turned yellow underneath. The water plant moved gently with the currents, and fresh water washed through the leaf tunnel. It brought oxygen to the egg and took away carbon dioxide, and the egg grew into a newt embryo. Adult newts and other predators hunting in the water above didn't see the newt embryo in its leaf curl, and the dragonfly larvae looking for food stayed in the mud around the stem.

After a few days, the newt embryo had grown long and skinny and had to curl up to fit inside the egg. It was still brown on top and yellow on the bottom, and it flipped from side to side. The jelly around the outside picked up bits of algae and mud from the moving water and began to look dirty.

A shiny black diving beetle, using two of its legs like oars, zoomed into the leaf tunnel and started to pull at the jelly with its sharp jaws. But when it got close to the newt embryo, it backed away as if it suddenly tasted something bad. The beetle slipped out of the tunnel and sped away. It zigzagged through the water looking for something else to eat.

After a month in the leaf tunnel, the newt embryo was only as big as a grain of rice, but she did have a head, eyes, three pairs of small lacy gills on her neck, and two stubby front legs. She hatched into a newt larva, or tadpole, by slithering through what was left of the jelly. She clung with her mouth to the edge of the leaf tunnel, balanced with the short front leg stubs, and let her tail drift in the water currents. Her heart pumped blood through her gills, taking oxygen from the water and releasing carbon dioxide. After a while, she let go of the leaf, drifted down to the bottom, and settled into the soft mud. Her narrow body wiggled through the mud, where her swimming movements could not be seen.

Nearby, a dragonfly larva shot out its hinged lower jaw and trapped a frog tadpole. The newt larva slipped away and rested, her red gills outstretched.

Later, she began to creep through the mud, nudging everything in her path with her nose. When a prey animal smelled right and wasn't too big, the newt larva opened her mouth quickly and sucked in the prey and lots of water. Then she closed her mouth, catching the prey with her tiny teeth, and squirted the water out past her gills. She ate mostly other larvae—soft-bodied larvae of insects—and tiny snails and clams.

A mosquito larva floated high above her at the surface of the pond, snorkeling through a breathing tube on its tail. A water beetle whizzed past, and the mosquito larva dived down to the mud by wriggling its body. Its speed carried it well into the mud, and it stopped right in front of the newt larva, who stepped forward and sucked its head into her mouth. The mosquito

larva's tail thrashed back and forth, but the little newt larva hung on to the biggest meal she had ever caught.

She found lots of prey in the rich mud and grew fast. When she was two months old, she was a little more than half an inch long, big enough to almost stretch across a penny. Elbows and little bumps for fingers appeared on her front legs, and back leg stubs poked out and helped in balancing. The three pairs of gills branched out in bright red brushes that were bigger than her head. Her body became heavier and rounder, and a crest of skin grew from just behind her head, down her back and tail, and around under her tail to her back legs. She swam like a snake, moving her body in quick, S-shaped curves, and the crest worked like a whole body flipper to make her go faster.

One day as she was creeping toward a tiny red worm, she felt water movements with a special row of sensitive cells along the sides of her body. She took another cautious step, but the vibrations were getting stronger and faster. She flipped her tail and dived deep into the mud. A baby snapping turtle, just a bit bigger than a quarter, crashed into the mud on top of her, flailing with its sharp claws and sending up an underwater cloud. Fat bullfrog tadpoles scattered in all directions, and the newt larva squirmed deeper, feeling the weight and thrashing of the turtle on top of her. The turtle scratched the mud, throwing up more clouds, but the newt stayed quiet against the hard sand under the mud. After a while, the turtle swam away, trailing streams of mud and a few water plant roots. The newt larva waited a long time before moving up through the mud to start hunting again.

As her legs got longer, the newt larva folded them back against her body while swimming fast, and now she became bold enough to swim up into the clear water. She still found most of her food in the mud, but sometimes she could catch a mosquito larva above the mud. She could also rest on the mud surface instead of burrowing in. She stuck out all four legs for balance and swayed in the water currents. Here she could hunt by sight as well as by feel and smell. When a water flea or a snail moved in front of her, she sucked it in. Most hungry predators didn't try to eat her. Even as an egg, she had produced poisonous chemicals that smelled and tasted bad. Some newt larvae in the pond did get eaten by snapping turtles, dragonfly larvae, adult newts, and bullfrogs, but the older the newts get, the more of the poison they make in tiny skin glands.

A young water snake cruised by and flicked its tongue a few times toward the resting newt larva. The snake's tongue touched her on the neck. The newt pulled her legs underneath her body and stood up tall on the tips of her toes, rocking from side to side. After a few more tongue flicks, the snake moved off. A few seconds later, it grabbed a bullfrog tadpole in its jaws. Mud rose in clouds as the snake and tadpole struggled. The snake pulled the tadpole up on the bank and the mud settled.

Spring moved into summer. The pond water stayed warm, even at night. Insect larvae that had escaped being eaten changed to adults and flew away on bright shiny wings, and the newt larva ate more snails and clams. But food was getting harder to find down in the mud.

The newt larva now had five toes on each back foot and four toes on the front feet. Her swimming crest and gills shrank, and her body became rounder. Inside her chest, two tiny lungs had started to grow.

One day she swam up to the surface with smooth, S-shaped waves of her tail, legs folded back against her sides. Her nose broke through to air for the first time. She drew in enough breath to keep floating with just her nostrils out of the water and stretched out all four legs for balance. The new lungs took oxygen from the fresh air.

Then she breathed out some of the air and sank down to the mud again. As she drifted lightly in the water currents, her lungs continued to remove oxygen from the air inside them and to release carbon dioxide into it. The gills still took in oxygen too, but much less. After a few minutes' rest, she swam back up to the surface, breathed out the old air, and drew in a new supply.

For several days the sun shone so brightly that even the animals down in the mud felt it. The water became warmer all over, and the cold spots faded away. The top few inches of water were warmer than ever before, and sometimes after a breath the newt larva would hang at the surface, four legs spread for balance, turning her head back and forth to watch for predators. Then she would flick her tail and ripple back down to the mud.

She rested and hunted and took trips up to the surface to breathe. Her tail, which used to be shaped like a fish tail, became rounder, and her skin grew rough little bumps all over. Eight red spots appeared on each side in an uneven line, and her dark green skin color turned lighter and browner. Her skin glands produced more of the protective chemicals, and hunting snakes didn't even come close to her anymore. She was now more than an inch long, big enough to stretch across a quarter and hang over both edges.

7

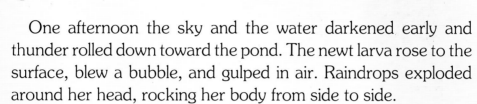

One afternoon the sky and the water darkened early and thunder rolled down toward the pond. The newt larva rose to the surface, blew a bubble, and gulped in air. Raindrops exploded around her head, rocking her body from side to side.

She sank down into the mud and settled on the tips of her toes. She turned her head from side to side and rubbed her snout on a stick. A thin white layer of skin started to peel off, and with more rubbing, she pulled the old skin back over her head, away from her gills, and down her legs. She twisted around, snapped at pieces of skin, and ate them. A leech was stuck to the skin on her back and she ate it too. She stepped out of the skin on one front leg while pulling with the other foot, like someone peeling off long, tight gloves.

She writhed her body, bit at her back legs, and rubbed against the bark on the stick. Finally all the skin came off and she ate the last pieces. Her new skin was lighter than the old one, and the orange spots were brighter. Then she swam up to the surface, took a big breath, and stayed there, nose out. The rain came harder, making craters in the water that were bigger than the newt's body.

She swam toward shore and came to a shallow, sandy place where she could stand on the bottom and breathe at the same time. Raindrops pounded all around, splashing behind the newt but whispering on the wet leaves in front. She moved toward the softer sounds until her nose pushed against the spongy plants of the pond bank.

With one last swimming stroke of her tail, the newt larva left the water and began her life on land as an air-breathing eft. Her gills, which had floated and waved behind her head in the water, sagged into dark red lumps on her neck. She climbed up a mossy rock on the bank, tumbled back, and tried again, this time tumbling over the other side. Scrambling through thick grass and weeds, she wriggled quietly behind a large bullfrog sitting on the pond bank. She bumped into a rock, went around, bumped into a log and went over, always going away from the pond.

The walking got easier. Soft pine needles, mosses, and ferns covered the ground. Tree trunks got in the way, but the eft could climb up over their roots, slide down the other side, and take up her straight path again. She moved quickly for several steps and then stopped motionless, head up, alert while resting. Her body twisted back and forth while she crawled, a bit like a snake's, because she always stepped forward with one front leg and pushed back with the hind leg of the same side at the same time.

After each rest, the eft hurried on again, until she was ten feet from the pond bank—well out of the hunting range of the bullfrogs that patrolled the shoreline. She crawled under a piece of bark, wrapped her tail around her nose, and rested in the cool darkness. The rain kept falling.

Before dawn she backed out of her hiding place and set off in the same direction, away from the pond. The rain had stopped, but the air was wet with cool mist. The skin under the eft's throat moved up and down, pushing air back to her lungs. She also absorbed some oxygen through her wet skin, but her gills had shrunk so that they could hardly be seen.

The clouds cleared and sunlight flowed through the forest, making the red spots on the eft glow like rubies. Drops of water hanging from the tips of leaves sparkled.

A fly landed in front of the eft and started to clean its first set of legs by rubbing them together. The eft shot out her tongue and pulled the squirming fly against the two rows of tiny, sharp teeth on the roof of her mouth. The eft chewed three or four times, crunching with her jaws and holding the fly against the roof of her mouth with her tongue. Then she swallowed, pulling in her eyes to help push the fly down her throat.

The eft's back and sides dried in the sunshine and looked as if some orange paint had mixed with the brown of her skin. The red spots looked even brighter, and each one had a thin black rim. She needed to keep her skin damp to absorb oxygen, and she crawled away from the sunlight and started to climb a shaded hill covered with wet leaves.

Finally the eft pulled herself over the top onto a mound of green moss in full sun. She pumped air into her lungs with her throat and absorbed more oxygen from the water in the moss. Her breathing rate slowed, and she started off again to find shade.

Suddenly she was hit by a round sticky glob. First it smashed her down against the moss and then lifted her high in the air. She thrashed her body and tail, but couldn't get loose. She had been caught by a toad that had noticed her movement. The toad's tongue pulled the little eft into a mouth like a pink cavern. Its jaws snapped shut and pierced the eft's back as the sticky tongue dragged her farther in. The protective poison oozed from the eft's skin and mixed with the toad's saliva. The eft started to slide down toward the toad's stomach, pushed by the bottoms of the toad's eyes as it blinked. Digestive enzymes began to burn her skin. But then the toad tasted the poison. It opened its jaws as wide as its pink mouth would stretch and vomited the eft back onto the bed of moss.

She scrambled away and crawled under a log that was soft and wet underneath. She pushed into the crumbly wood and wrapped her tail around her snout.

The toad reached up with one foot and clawed at its tongue, falling over sideways with the effort. Then it clawed its tongue with the other front foot, falling the other way. It leaned forward and wiped its mouth on the moss, snapped its jaws a few times, and clawed at its mouth again. Then it hopped away, stopping after every few hops to wipe its mouth on the ground.

The sun dried the forest floor, and the leaves and pine needles became crisp. But the rotten wood stayed wet. The eft curled tighter, keeping her skin damp.

Two days later the wounds from the toad's jaws and stomach enzymes were healed, and on a foggy evening the eft crawled out. Her skin was more orange than brown now, especially on her head and back, and the poison glands became more active. The brighter orange was a warning to predators to stay away, that even though she was small and slow, she was not good to eat.

Mushrooms had popped up on the forest floor after the rainstorm. The eft came to a big soft one leaning against the base of a tree. Two other, larger efts were there, solid orange, eating maggots that had hatched in the fleshy top of the mushroom. The small eft climbed up and joined them, poking into the mushroom until she felt a maggot, catching it on her tongue, and swallowing with gulps and eye blinks. The other efts crawled off, bellies dragging. The small eft ate maggots until her stomach was full and tight, then crawled off in a different direction, found a wet log, and rested there during two weeks of dry weather.

Another rainstorm. The eft crawled out, even before water soaked under the log. The leaves on the ground were still dry, and some danced and rustled with the wind that came with the rain. But the heavy raindrops soon settled the leaves, and the eft set out under fern umbrellas.

At first the rainwater disappeared into the ground, but then it started collecting in puddles and running down rocks and slopes. The eft ate two earthworms that crept out of their flooded tunnels. Then she moved on, still traveling away from the pond where she had hatched. Now she was bright orange, head to tail, and the red spots glowed. When she was out on foggy or rainy days, hungry blue jays would notice her movement, swoop down for a closer look, and fly away. Toads usually ignored the bright orange eft, but if a toad came close, the eft rose up on her toes, lowered her head, and waved her tail slowly back and forth in warning. The toad would back up and then hop off. Garter snakes came close, flicked their tongues at the eft, and then slid away. The eft never tried to run—she either rose up on her toes or kept walking.

The days got shorter and the rain got colder. On some days, even a long, soaking rain wouldn't persuade the eft to leave a comfortable rotten log. She ate well during her first summer, and her belly was round because of the yellow fat stored inside.

One foggy autumn day, she nosed around the roots of a tree stump and found a soft place where a root had rotted deep into the ground. She followed the root, pushing and digging into wood that had almost become soil. She continued down to a spot that was moist and cool and curled up tight with her tail wrapped around her snout.

When the frost came, she was safe and still, ready for her first hibernation.

The ground became hard with ice crystals, thawed to mud, froze again, and then settled under a blanket of snow. The stump also sheltered a sleeping chipmunk and its winter store of nuts, hundreds of tightly wrapped insect and spider eggs, some beetle grubs,

and a centipede curled up in a ball. Deep in one root, termites chewed off bits of wood and carried them down to a warm chamber where the termite queen laid eggs all winter. On sunny days a red squirrel brought acorns to the stump and peeled them, covering the stump with a mound of shell pieces. The squirrel felt safe there; it could see in all directions and knew where to leap up a good climbing tree if a fox appeared. Deep in the ground, the eft slept for five months, safe from snow, sleet, and wind.

Warm spring rains finally wakened the eft. She crawled up the rotted tree root and ate some earthworms along the way. She pushed through flattened oak leaves and out into a drizzly rain. Bloodroot and jack-in-the-pulpit flowers growing at the base of the stump danced when raindrops hit them. The eft's body was as cool as the wet earth, and she had only enough energy to move a few steps at a time. After crossing two small logs and a patch of moss, she crawled under a piece of bark and rested.

She was longer and thinner than she had been at the end of her first summer. Her head seemed too big for her body. As the spring sun warmed the forest floor, she nosed around under leaves or waited perfectly still in wet places. She ate fat white grubs, careless flies, spiders, and earthworms that crawled up through the leaves. Under one log, she found a broken termite tunnel and picked off termites as they scurried across the opening. When the termites repaired the hole with lumps of mud, the eft set off to find something else.

She hunted whenever it was warm and wet enough, and her body filled out even while she was getting longer. Spring moved into summer, and dry weather kept the eft out of sight during the day.

One foggy dawn she moved down a hill toward a forest pond that was almost dried up. Tadpoles and insect larvae crowded in the last patch of water, which was too shallow for them to swim in without breaking the surface. Other efts and several frogs and toads were already there, standing on the mud at the edge of the shrinking pool, snapping wiggling prey out of the water. The eft joined them and stayed until her belly bulged and dragged on the ground. Thrushes and ovenbirds flew out of the fog to catch meals for their nestlings as the amphibians dragged themselves to hiding places.

The next morning the pond was smaller, and the eft took her place at the edge and filled her belly again. Later that day the sun dried the pool into hard mud, and the birds picked the last tadpoles and insect larvae from the surface.

That night the eft crawled up the hill on the other side of the mud patch and moved along a ridge. Just before sunrise she crawled down the other side and found a fallen tree with loose bark. She squeezed between the bark and the wood, breaking white strands of fungus and scattering a family of centipedes. The eft went as far as her full belly would allow and curled up in a damp spot. She stayed there for four weeks of drought, pushing farther under the bark as she got skinnier. The fungus threads dried up and crumbled, and the eft had to squeeze herself deeper and deeper to keep moist enough to absorb oxygen.

Finally it rained, torrents of rain that came with thunder, lightning, and water rushing down all surfaces. The tree bark swelled and the eft squirmed out. She started walking, still away from her larval pond, crossing rivulets and slipping on wet moss. She walked and rested, walked and rested, as long as it rained. Summer was almost over, and she found nothing to eat. The next day was cool, and she rested under a log.

It was a good log, big and soft underneath, with large chunks of wood crumbling into soil. The eft looked for food when it was warm and wet enough, but came back to the log each time she needed shelter. She found a few earthworms and snails to eat, but she had no chance to really fill her stomach again. It was early fall, and the nights were too cold for cold-blooded animals to hunt.

Dry weather came, and she snuggled under the crumbly wood. One night a heavy dew settled on the log and froze. The frost sparkled when the first sun rays hit it, and the eft settled into her second hibernation.

It was a hard winter. Wind blew away the snow blanket, and the cold reached down into the log. Many amphibians and insects died as they hibernated that winter because of the dry cold and because they hadn't been able to store enough body fat during the drought. But finally, after a few false thaws, spring and warm rain came again. The eft crawled out and used her last stored energy for a long hunting trip. Her backbone made a sharp line down her back and her sides looked hollow. She stayed thin until summer, when the nights were warm enough for efts to be out.

She still moved away from her larval pond. One night, walking in a gentle rain, she came to a roadside of hard sand and gravel. She climbed up steep, sharp rocks and stepped out onto the pavement. It was still warm from the day, and she walked with her head and tail held high. A young grasshopper with no wings landed right in front of her and she ate it.

The eft stopped on the yellow line in the middle of the road. Blinding white lights rushed toward her from both directions. She stood high on her toes, lowered her head, and waved her tail. Her orange skin glowed in the headlights.

With a roar, the two cars passed each other. A wall of water mixed with sand and pebbles from the tires knocked the eft off her feet and tumbled her along the road until she finally stopped near the edge. She scrambled to get right side up and slid on her belly like a snake to escape into the weeds.

The new place on the other side of the road had a beaver pond and a lot of marshy, damp areas. The eft could hunt in the wet moss even during the day, and she found lots of flies, wingless grasshoppers, beetle grubs, caterpillars, snails, and worms. Her body became rounder and she grew longer. She rested under moss clumps, hunted, and rested again. After a few weeks, she was almost as long as the adult newts that lived in her larval pond.

On another rainy night, late in July, she turned back toward the road. She crawled up the gravel bank two hours before sunrise. No cars came, and she crossed with her head and tail held high over the wet pavement. After scrambling down the other road bank, she started up the first of many hills that lay between her and the pond where she hatched.

The nights were warm and she could travel in the fog until it burned off in the August sun. Then she rested under wet leaves or damp logs. She hurried across ridge tops; it was drier there. In valleys she stayed near water for a few days to catch food. Her back looked a little browner now, and the bright orange of her sides and belly faded. A ridge grew along the top of her tail. The red spots on her sides still glowed.

Sometimes she had to wait for several days for rain or heavy fog, but whenever the ground and air were damp enough, she traveled. For six weeks she crawled toward her larval pond, climbing steep hillsides and tumbling down over logs. She stayed away from sunny open places, but sometimes she had to cross rocky ledges to keep going in the right direction. A part of her brain worked like a compass, and she migrated on nearly the same route she had followed away from the pond. Her back and sides lost more of the orange color, and as soon as sunlight filtered through the trees each morning, she disappeared under a log or leaves.

One foggy night in late September, she came down a hillside and onto a flat, moist area of rich grass and moss. She slipped under a log that smelled familiar and comfortable, and she found three snails to eat. Her journey as an eft was over. She was luckier than some efts. Her pond was clear and clean, and the tall trees still sheltered it from wind and too much sun. It had not

been drained or bulldozed, and no houses or roads had been built during the two years she spent wandering in the forest. It was still a good place for an eft to grow up into an adult newt.

The next night it rained, and she crept quietly toward the pond bank. The bullfrogs sat like stuffed armchairs, pumping their chins up and down, but they didn't see her moving so carefully behind them that she didn't touch grass blades. She plopped into the pond and swam with her tail down to the dark bottom. The water was very cold.

And it kept getting colder as the nights got longer. The newt ate a few clams, but spent most of her time exploring the mud near the bank and finding soft places where she could burrow down and not bump into rocks. The bullfrogs also found places in the mud. First quiet and then ice settled around the edge of the pond, and the newt nestled into a soft burrow between two rocks. She curled up in a tight ball and slept. She couldn't breathe, but her skin absorbed enough oxygen from the wet mud to keep her alive. This was her third hibernation, and now, as an adult newt, she would never wander on land again, though she could survive if her pond dried up during a late summer drought. Most newts live for two or three years as adults, and once they have returned to the water, they find all their food, hiding places, and hibernation spots in or near one pond. The migrating part of their life is over.

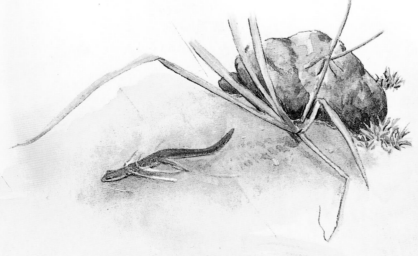

Ice and snow covered the pond, and the black water became silent and still. Storms brought wind, sleet, and more snow. Animals stayed in the mud for five months and did not stir until the last ice melted and warmth from the thin spring sun seeped into their burrows. Then, very slowly, frogs, newts and other salamanders, water insects, turtles, snails, and other pond animals crept out and crawled to the warmest parts of the pond. The newt moved slowly too, but she found a few things to eat and discovered good hiding places near the pond bank. Her back and sides were greenish brown, and the pale yellow of her belly flashed in the water when she swam. Her tail had grown a new crest, and waving it just once or twice, she shot through the water. The rough bumps on her skin smoothed out, and all that was left of her eft orange were the bright spots along her sides.

The nights were still cold and frosty, but spring peepers called from the trees. Spotted salamanders from many parts of the forest left their cold mud hiding places and met in the coolest part of the pond, shaded by the brown hillside. These salamanders are much bigger than newts and are black with large yellow spots. After mating, the female spotted salamanders laid large clumps of eggs around underwater sticks. The jelly looked like bunches of skinless grapes with no stems, with the eggs inside each grape like a seed. The spotted salamanders left the pond and crept under logs or moss near the water to rest. Then each one set out in a different direction through the forest. They wouldn't be back again until next winter's ice left the pond.

One morning, warmer sun rays flickered down through the cool water, and a breeze kept little waves moving slowly across the pond. The bullfrog tadpoles were already out in the sunny shallow places, their fat bodies rolling gently back and forth like soft marbles with tails on one side. On a muddy patch on the shore, a clump of earth moved and the edge of a box turtle shell appeared backing out of the cool mud. It moved one hind leg slowly through the air and then pulled it back into the shell. The mud oozed down and covered the turtle shell again.

Newts drifted in from the deep water where they had spent the night. They looked like green shadows on the bottom, and the water was cloudy enough to make the red spots almost invisible. They moved smoothly, one swimming stroke at a time, then a long rest, then another stroke with the tail.

A black, shiny crow landed near the turtle's mud lump. The lump sank as the turtle clamped its shell closed with a hiss. The sunning tadpoles exploded into action, bumping into one another and splashing their tails above the water surface. They scampered away, their marble bodies wobbling in front of frantic tails. Some plunged into nearby mud and some dashed for the deep water. One tried to squeeze into a crack under a rock that was too small and finally disappeared into a patch of mud next to the rock. The line of newts that had been moving toward shore stopped, and the next swimming strokes were all away from shore.

The crow stepped into the water, pecked at the mud a few times, and then spread its wings. The newts watched as the crow flapped away with water dripping from its toes. The turtle's mud lump rose a little as if it were breathing.

The newt swam close to shore, close enough to feel a warm layer of water. She sat motionless for five minutes. A few tadpoles slipped by to shallower sunning spots. Spring sunlight poured through the leafless branches.

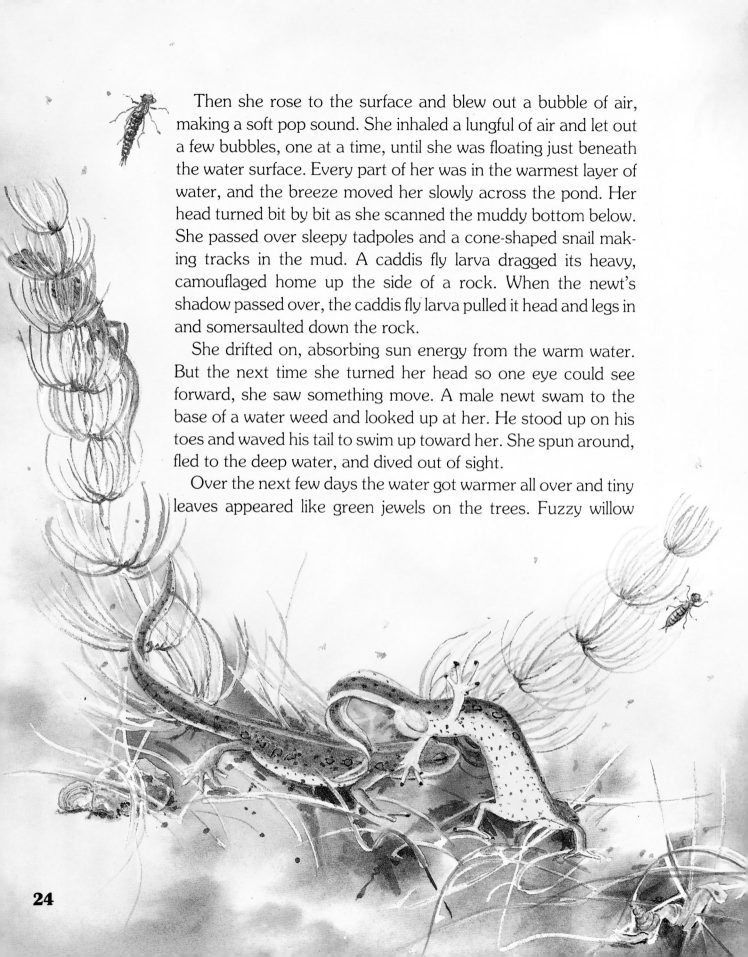

Then she rose to the surface and blew out a bubble of air, making a soft pop sound. She inhaled a lungful of air and let out a few bubbles, one at a time, until she was floating just beneath the water surface. Every part of her was in the warmest layer of water, and the breeze moved her slowly across the pond. Her head turned bit by bit as she scanned the muddy bottom below. She passed over sleepy tadpoles and a cone-shaped snail making tracks in the mud. A caddis fly larva dragged its heavy, camouflaged home up the side of a rock. When the newt's shadow passed over, the caddis fly larva pulled it head and legs in and somersaulted down the rock.

She drifted on, absorbing sun energy from the warm water. But the next time she turned her head so one eye could see forward, she saw something move. A male newt swam to the base of a water weed and looked up at her. He stood up on his toes and waved his tail to swim up toward her. She spun around, fled to the deep water, and dived out of sight.

Over the next few days the water got warmer all over and tiny leaves appeared like green jewels on the trees. Fuzzy willow catkins dropped yellow pollen on the water. The box turtle backed all the way out of its mud tunnel and wandered into the woods, looking for mushrooms. The newt explored the shoreline of the pond, swimming a few strokes and then resting and watching.

Across the pond, the spotted salamander eggs had grown into embryos. They flipped back and forth in their large clumps of jelly.

The flipping motions caught the newt's eye as she swam by. She dived down and tore the jelly with her front feet and then snapped at the tough membranes surrounding the salamander embryos. She ate salamander embryos in one clump right down to the stick, leaving ragged pieces of jelly floating in the water. A few embryos underneath the stick were still flipping as the newt swam away to the sunny side of the pond. Her belly was round and full.

Two days later, the newt had digested the salamander embryos, but her belly still looked round. She drifted into shallow sunny water. A large male newt swam at the water surface, looking in all directions. His swimming crest was much bigger than hers, and he had rough black pads on his hind legs and toes. When he saw her, he dived to her side and rubbed his chin over the top of her snout. Then he moved in front of her and started dancing. He stood on his toes and moved his hind legs and tail from side to side, as if he were twirling a Hula Hoop sideways. She turned away and started to leave, but he swam toward her and circled her neck with his hind legs. The black patches on his legs and toes kept her from slipping away. Then he twisted his body around and rubbed his cheeks and chin over her snout. Both newts thrashed their tails and raised a small cloud of mud. Other male newts came over to investigate, but drifted away as the mating pair settled quietly on the bottom.

They stayed clasped together for two hours. Then the male let go of her neck, released a few air bubbles, and shuffled away from her, holding his tail to one side. She followed him, touching the base of his tail with her snout. After a few steps, the male stopped and produced a spermatophore, a glob of jelly. The spermatophore stuck to a rock and stood like a little cup. On top of the spermatophore was a tiny white package of sperm cells. The male newt crept on a little farther with the female newt still following. When she was right over the spermatophore, he turned and stopped her by standing sideways across her path. She took the sperm package into her body, and then both newts swam up to the water surface for a lungful of air.

Seven days later, the female newt moved to a quiet part of the pond, where there were few other newts and no fish. She swam slowly along the bottom, looking for hiding places for her eggs—underneath sticks, in cracks of rocks, and especially on the stems of water weeds. As each egg passed out of her body, she released some sperm from the sperm package stored in her body to fertilize the egg.

She laid eggs, hunted, rested, basked in shallow water, and then went back to lay more eggs. One day she swam to the shaded side of the pond and moved through the cool water. Spotted salamander larvae scampered away from her. She caught one and ate it, but the others had grown too big for her and she didn't chase them. She rose to the surface. She took a gulp of air and swam back to the muddy bottom with a few strong tail strokes. Her nose came to the stem of a water weed. She twisted her body around it, grasped the stem with both hind feet, and laid an egg surrounded by clear jelly. She pulled a leaf down and made a little tunnel around the egg. Then she swam to the bottom, nosing at the mud and a few rotting sticks. She found some tiny clams, ate them, folded her legs back against her body, and swam away through the cloudy water.

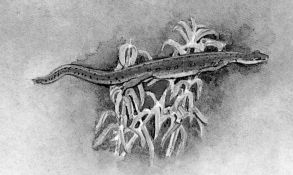

INDEX

DATE			